This book belongs to

_____

A B C D

H I J

O P Q R

V W X

This book is dedicated to my children - Mikey, Kobe, and Jojo.

Copyright © 2023 Grow Grit Press LLC. All rights reserved. No part of this book may be reproduced in any form without permission in writing from the publisher. Please send bulk order requests to info@ninjalifehacks.tv

Paperback ISBN: 978-1-63731-721-1
Hardcover ISBN: 978-1-63731-723-5
eBook ISBN: 978-1-63731-722-8

Printed and bound in the USA.
NinjaLifeHacks.tv

Ninja Life Hacks®
by Mary Nhin

A ninja knows the ABCs of feelings,
And uses them day and night.

A ninja acts with honor, courage and bravery,
And tries to do what's right!

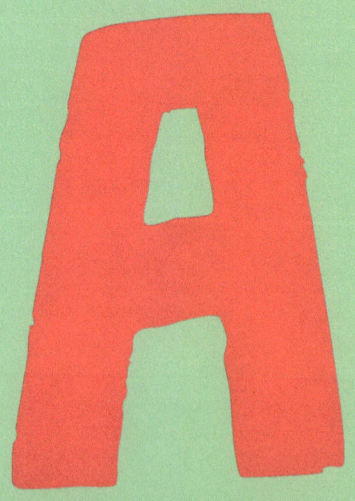 is for **Angry**,
When you really want to scream.

B is for **Brave**,
Many challenges aren't as scary as they seem.

C is for **Curious**,
Always wanting to learn and explore.

D is for **Diversity** and inclusion,
Of all cultures, races, and more!

E is for **Earth**,
Reusing and recycling to care for our planet.

F is for **Feelings**,
Emotions that happen even if you don't plan it.

 is for **Grateful**,
By showing how much you care.

 is for **Humble**,
And never wanting to compare.

I is for **Innovative**,
Carving paths not taken before.

J is for **Jealous**,
Wanting what others have ... and more!

K is for **Kind**,
Always lending a helping hand.

L

is for **Listening**,
Paying attention to understand.

M is for **Motivated**,
Getting up to try, each and every day.

N

is for **Nervous**,

Being worried about what to do or say.

O is for **Organized**,
Putting each thing in its place.

Q is for **Quiet**,
Using tippy toes and a ninja voice.

R is for **Respectful**,
Letting other ninjas have their choice.

S

is for **Sharing**,
Especially when others need supplies or food.

T is for **Tired**,
And remember – being sleepy affects your mood.

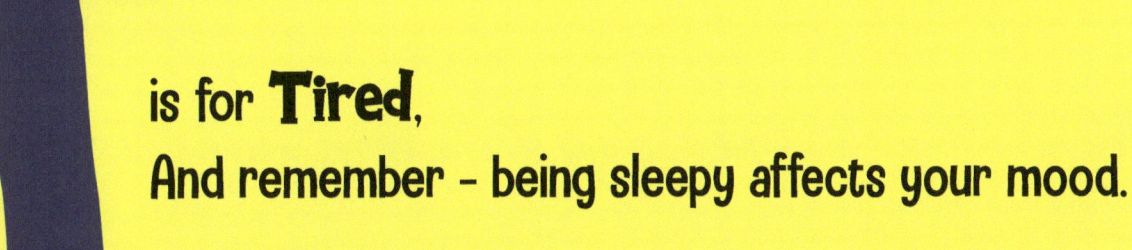

U is for **Unplugged**, Discovering all the beauty in nature!

V is for **Visionary**,
Taking bold steps to be a creator.

W is for **Worry**,
Wanting things to not look so bleak.

X is for eXhausted,
Feeling so tired it makes you weak.

Y is for **Young**,
No matter your age, feeling young is a great start.

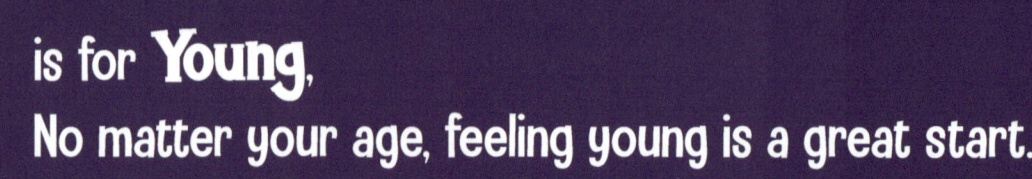

And Z? **Z** is for **Zen**,
Finding the calm inside your heart.

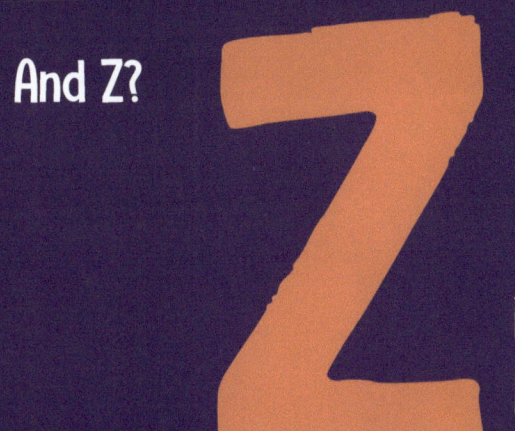

A B C D
H I J
O P Q R
V W X

Continue the learning with our fun lesson plans which include superpower skills practice, STEM activity, craft, and more! Visit ninjalifehacks.tv

 @marynhin @officialninjalifehacks
#NinjaLifeHacks

 Ninja Life Hacks

 Mary Nhin   Ninja Life Hacks

 @officialninjalifehacks

www.ingramcontent.com/pod-product-compliance
Lightning Source LLC
Chambersburg PA
CBHW041523070526
44585CB00002B/60